Gaby's Garden

AF668477

Om KIDZ

An imprint of Om Books International

Om Kidz | Om Books International

Reprinted in 2023

Corporate & Editorial Office
A-12, Sector 64, Noida 201 301
Uttar Pradesh, India
Phone: +91 120 477 4100
Email: editorial@ombooks.com
Website: www.ombooksinternational.com

Sales Office
107, Ansari Road, Darya Ganj
New Delhi 110 002, India
Phone: +91 11 4000 9000
Email: sales@ombooks.com
Website: www.ombooks.com

ISBN: 978-93-52760-25-1

Printed in India

10 9 8 7 6 5 4 3 2

Gaby's Garden

Paste your photograph here

My name is

____

Gaby is a **good girl**.
She loves to play in
her **garden**.

Gaby loves her **garden**,
it is so **green** and full of **grass**.
There are little **green** shrubs
in the **garden** too.

Gaby's garden has a **great** big tree in the middle.

The tree **gives** shade
on a hot summer day.

Gaby waters her plants every day. She wants them to **grow** big like the tree.

Gaby is **glad** to see the **green** leaves every morning. "**Good** morning!" she **greets** all the plants of the **garden**.

One day, **Gaby goes** into her **garden**. All the leaves on the plants are torn and broken.

"Where did the leaves **go**?" she wonders.

The **green grass** on the **ground** is also missing in some places. **Gaby** runs into the house and calls her **Grandma**.

"**Grandma**, look! So many leaves in the garden are gone! Only the leaves on the trees are left.

Who could have done this?"
asks **Gaby**.

Grandma thinks hard. She does not know for sure what has happened. But she can **guess**. “We will know tomorrow,” **Grandma** says to **Gaby**.

Next day, **Gaby** does not **go** into the **garden**. She stays inside the house. She plays a **game** with her **Grandpa** instead.

All of a sudden, **Grandma** calls **Gaby** to the window. **Gaby** looks outside. There is a big, fat **goat** in the **garden**!

It is eating the **grass** on the **ground** and the **green** leaves as well. Now **Gaby** knows what happened to the leaves.

With **Grandpa's** help, **Gaby** puts up a fence around her **garden**. The **goat** can't eat the leaves anymore. Next summer, **Gaby's garden** is **green** and leafy again!

Know your words

Naming words

Gaby	grass	game
girl	ground	Grandpa
garden	Grandma	goat

Describing words

good	great	glad
green		

Doing words

gives	goes	go
grow	gone	guess
greets		

Fill in the blanks.

G__rl

Gr__ss

G__ __t

G__n__

Gr__ndm__

G__rd__n

Spot 5 differences between the two pictures..

Join the dots to show who is eating Gaby's plants. Colour it.